Mr Badger

from
The Wind in the Willows

Written by
KENNETH GRAHAME

Abridged and illustrated by
INGA MOORE

TED SMART

Mr Badger

They waited patiently for what seemed a very long time, stamping in the snow to keep their feet warm. At last they heard the sound of slow shuffling footsteps approaching the door from the inside. It seemed, as the Mole remarked to the Rat, like someone walking in carpet slippers that were too large for him and down-at-heel; which was intelligent of Mole, because that was exactly what it was.

There was the noise of a bolt shot back, and the door opened a few inches, to show a long snout and a pair of sleepy eyes.

"Now, the *very* next time this happens," said a gruff and suspicious voice, "I shall be exceedingly angry. Who is it *this* time, disturbing people on such a night? Speak up!"

"O, Badger," cried the Rat, "let us in, please. It's me, Rat, and my friend Mole, and we've lost our way in the snow."

"Ratty!" exclaimed the Badger, in quite a different voice. "Come along in, both of you. Why, you must be perished. Well, I never! Lost in the snow! And in the Wild Wood too, at this time of night!"

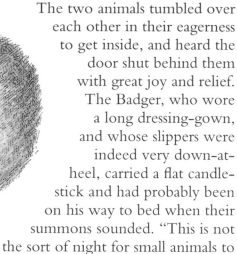

The two animals tumbled over each other in their eagerness to get inside, and heard the door shut behind them with great joy and relief. The Badger, who wore a long dressing-gown, and whose slippers were indeed very down-at-heel, carried a flat candle-stick and had probably been on his way to bed when their summons sounded. "This is not the sort of night for small animals to be out," he said. "I'm afraid you've been up to some of your pranks again, Ratty."

He shuffled on in front of them, carrying the light, and they followed him down a long, and to tell the truth, decidedly shabby passage, into a sort of a hall, out of which they could see other passages branching mysteriously. There were doors as well – stout oaken doors. One of these the Badger flung open, and they found themselves in all the glow and warmth of a large fire-lit kitchen.

The kindly Badger thrust them down on a settle to toast themselves at the fire, and bade them remove their wet coats and boots. Then he fetched them dressing-gowns and slippers, and bathed the Mole's shin with warm water and mended the cut with sticking-plaster till the whole thing was as good as new, if not better. Warm and dry at last, with weary legs propped up in front of them, it seemed to the storm-driven animals that the cold and trackless Wild Wood just left outside was miles and miles away, and all that they had suffered in it a half-forgotten dream.

When at last they were thoroughly toasted, the Badger summoned them to the table. They had felt pretty hungry before, but when they saw the supper spread for them, it seemed only a question of what they should attack first where all was so attractive, and whether the other things would wait till they had time to give them attention. Conversation was impossible for a long time; and when it was resumed, it was that regrettable sort that results from talking with your mouth full. The Badger did not mind that sort of thing at all, nor did he take any notice of elbows on the table, or everybody speaking at once. As the animals told their story, he did not seem surprised or shocked at anything. He never said, "I told you so," or, "Just what I always said," or remarked that they ought to have done so-and-so, or ought not to have done something else. The Mole began to feel very friendly towards him.

Supper finished, they gathered round the glowing embers of the great fire, and thought how jolly it was to be sitting up *so* late, and *so* full; and after they had chatted for a time, the Badger said, "Well, it's time we were all in bed." He conducted the two animals to a long room that seemed half bedchamber and half loft. The Badger's winter stores took up half the room, but the two little beds on the remainder of the floor looked soft and inviting, and the linen on them, though coarse, was clean and smelt beautifully of lavender; and the Mole and the Water Rat, shaking off their garments in some thirty seconds, tumbled in between the sheets in great joy and contentment.

The two tired animals
came down to breakfast
very late next morning,
and found a bright fire
burning in the kitchen,
and two young
hedgehogs sitting
on a bench at
the table, eating
oatmeal porridge
out of wooden
bowls.

The hedgehogs dropped their spoons and rose to their feet respectfully as the two entered.

"Sit down, sit down," said the Rat pleasantly, "and go on with your porridge. Where have you youngsters come from? Lost your way in the snow, I suppose?"

"Yes, please, sir," said the elder of the two hedgehogs. "Me and Billy was trying to find our way to school and we lost ourselves, sir, and Billy got frightened and took and cried, being young. And we happened up against Mr Badger's back door, and knocked, sir, for Mr Badger he's a kind-hearted gentleman, as everyone knows—"

"I understand," said the Rat, cutting himself some rashers of bacon, while the Mole dropped some eggs into a saucepan. "And what's the weather like outside? You needn't 'sir' me quite so much," he added.

"O, terrible bad, sir, terrible deep the snow is," said the hedgehog. "No getting out for you gentlemen today."

"Where's Mr Badger?" inquired the Mole.

"The master's gone into his study, sir," replied the hedgehog, "and said as how he was going to be particular busy this morning, and on no account was he to be disturbed."

The animals well knew that Badger, having eaten a hearty breakfast, had retired to his study and settled himself in an armchair with his legs on another and a red cotton handkerchief over his face, and was being "busy" in the usual way at this time of the year.

The front-door bell clanged loudly, and the Rat, who was very greasy with buttered toast, sent Billy, the smaller hedgehog, to see who it might be. There was a sound of much stamping in the hall, and presently Billy returned in front of the Otter, who threw himself on the Rat with a shout.

"Get off!" spluttered the Rat, with his mouth full.

"Thought I should find you here," said the Otter cheerfully. "They were all in a state along River Bank this morning. Rat never been home all night – nor Mole either – something dreadful must have happened, they said; and the snow had covered your tracks. But I knew when people were in any fix they mostly went to Badger, so I came straight here, through the Wild Wood. About halfway across I came on a rabbit sitting on a stump, cleaning his silly face. I managed to extract from him that Mole had been seen in the Wild Wood last night. It was the talk of the burrows, he said, how Mole, Mr Rat's particular friend, was in a bad fix; how he had lost his way, and 'They' were up and out hunting, and were chivvying him round and round. 'Why didn't you *do* something?' I asked. 'What, us?' he said: '*do* something? us rabbits?' So I cuffed him. There was nothing else to be done. At any rate, I had learnt something; and if I had had the luck to meet 'Them' I'd have learnt something more – or *they* would."

"Weren't you – er – nervous?" asked the Mole.

"Nervous?" The Otter laughed. "I'd give 'em nerves if any of them tried anything on with me. Here, Mole, fry me some slices of ham. I'm hungry, and I've any amount to say to Ratty here. Haven't seen him for an age."

So the good-natured Mole, having cut some slices of ham, set the hedgehogs to fry it, and returned to his own breakfast, while the Otter and the Rat talked river-shop.

A plate of fried ham had just been cleared and sent back for more, when the Badger entered, yawning and rubbing his eyes, and greeted them. "It must be getting on for luncheon time," he remarked to the Otter. "Better stop and have it with us. You must be hungry, this cold morning."

"Rather!" replied the Otter, winking at the Mole.

The hedgehogs, who were just beginning to feel hungry again after working so hard at their frying, looked timidly up at Mr Badger, but were too shy to say anything.

"You be off to your mother," said the Badger kindly. "I'll send someone with you to show you the way."

He gave them sixpence apiece and they went off.

Presently they all sat down to luncheon together. The Mole found himself next to Mr Badger, and, as the other two were still deep in river-gossip, he took the opportunity to tell Badger how home-like it all felt to him. "Once underground," he said, "you know exactly where you are. Nothing can happen to you, and nothing can get at you. Things go on all the same overhead, and you don't bother about 'em. When you want to, up you go, and there the things are, waiting for you."

The Badger beamed on him. "That's exactly what I say," he replied. "There's no security, or peace, except underground. Look at Rat, now. A couple of feet of flood-water, and he's got  to move into hired lodgings. Take Toad. I say nothing against Toad Hall; quite the best house in these parts, *as* a house. But supposing a fire breaks out – where's Toad? Supposing tiles are blown off, or windows get broken – where's Toad? No, up and out of doors is good enough to roam about and get one's living in; but underground – that's my idea of *home*!"

The Mole assented heartily; and the Badger got very friendly with him. "When lunch is over," he said, "I'll take you round this little place of mine."

Accordingly, when the other two had settled themselves into the chimney-corner and had started a heated argument on the subject of *eels*, the Badger lighted a lantern and bade the Mole follow him. Crossing the hall, they passed down one of the tunnels, and the wavering light gave glimpses on either side of rooms, some mere cupboards, others nearly as broad and imposing as Toad's dining-hall. A passage at right angles led into another corridor, and here the same thing was repeated. The Mole was staggered at the size of it all; at the length of the dim passages, the vaultings, the pillars, the arches.

"How on earth, Badger," said the Mole at last,

"did you do all this? It's astonishing!"

"It *would* be astonishing," said the Badger, "if I *had* done it. But as a matter of fact I did none of it – only cleaned out the passages, as I had need of them. You see, long ago, on the spot where the Wild Wood waves now, before ever it had planted itself and grown, there was a city – a city of people, you know. Here, where we are standing, they walked, and talked, and carried on their business. They were a powerful people, and rich, and great builders."

"But what has become of them all?" asked the Mole.

"Who can tell?" said the Badger. "People come – they stay for a while – and they go. But we remain. There were badgers here long before that same city ever came to be. And now there are badgers here again."

When they got back to the kitchen again, they found the Rat very restless. The underground atmosphere was getting on his nerves, and he seemed to be afraid that the river would run away if he wasn't there to look after it. He had his overcoat on, and his pistols thrust into his belt again. "Come along, Mole," he said. "We must get off while it's light. Don't want to spend another night in the Wild Wood."

"It'll be all right," said the Otter. "I'm coming with you. I know every path blindfold; and if there's a head to be punched, you can rely upon me to punch it."

"You needn't fret, Ratty," added the Badger. "My passages run further than you think, and I've bolt-holes to the edge of the wood in several directions, though I don't care for everybody to know about them. When you really have to go, you shall leave by one of my short cuts."

The Rat was still anxious to be off, so the Badger, taking up his lantern again, led the way along a damp and airless tunnel that wound and dipped for what seemed to be miles. At last daylight began to show itself through tangled growth overhanging the mouth of the passage; and the Badger, bidding them a hasty good-bye, pushed them through, made everything look as natural as possible again, with brushwood, and dead leaves, and retreated.

They found themselves standing on the very edge of the Wild Wood. Rocks and brambles and tree-roots behind them; in front, a great space of fields, hemmed by lines of hedges black on the snow, and, far ahead, a glint of the familiar old river, while the wintry sun hung red and low on the horizon. They trailed out on a bee-line for a distant stile. Pausing there and looking back, they saw the whole of the Wild Wood, menacing, compact, grimly set in vast white surroundings; they turned and made for home, for firelight and the familiar things it played on, for the voice of the river they knew and trusted, that never made them afraid.

As he hurried along, the Mole saw clearly he was an animal of field and hedgerow, the ploughed furrow, the frequented pasture, the lane of evening lingerings, the cultivated garden-plot. For others the conflict that went with Nature in the rough; he must be wise, must keep to the places in which his lines were laid and which held adventure enough, in their way, to last for a lifetime.